MW00938196

DEDICATION

To Andrea

For writing a storybook love with me since the day we met and until the end of time, for choosing to believe unwaveringly in me, even when my own faith faltered, and for igniting my inner fire with a flame that cannot be put out.

And of course, let's not forget, for your patience in dealing with my daily excitement!

To Teta

For your constant reminder that age is simply a number that can never mask your inner youth.
I will remember you with each word that I read.

To Moni

For relentlessly pushing me to pursue my passion, against all odds, and for inspiring me to forever dream like a child.
Oh yea, and for breathing life, and color, into each and every page in this book!

An
Almond
All
Alone

Rami Jandali

Salted or seasoned,
Hazel or Chest,
Each and every nut
Is different from the rest.

Pecans are ridged,
Pistachios are shelled,
Most are small enough
To be eaten handheld.

Now let's move to the story
Of an unusual nut,
He was born to the Almonds
With a body half-cut.

His face lacked a smile,
Friends he had none,
All that was missing
Was a life filled with fun...

In a land called *Nuttopia*, there were nuts of all sorts,
Round ones, crinkled ones and some with small warts.
The Pecans so practical, respected for their flavor,
There were Walnuts and Hazelnuts, with a taste you can savor.

And of course, the Mighty Pistachios, some green and some brown,
Their shells were so stunning, you'd mistake each for a crown!
The Peanuts were salty, the Pine Nuts so thin,
Chestnuts, they're heavy, even tougher than a chin!

And last but not least, the Almonds were humble,
Hard on the outside, but easy to crumble.
Light-brown in color, oval in shape,
Soft to the touch and tasty in a crepe!

Each week one nut is honored, for doing good deeds,
Some shine in school, while others plant seeds,

The lucky winner would be roasted, underneath the sun,
To be packaged as a snack, or added to a sweet bun.

This honor was grand, nuts dreamt of their roast,
Whether glazed or unsweetened, or on the side of some toast.
But one member of the Almonds, his face filled with sorrow,
He knew he'd never win, not today nor tomorrow.

He was born half-bitten, his body part-gone,
No one paid any attention, he was looked at with a yawn.
He sat in the back, of each room he was in,
Who could love HIM, if only he had a twin!

Some days he just sat there, and watched the others play,
The sky above them was blue, but over him it was gray.
There had to be some talent, within the Almond's crushed core,
Perhaps it was his voice, could he sing with a roar?

One day he hobbled, towards a group of Pecans,
He'd find a way to win gold, not silver nor bronze.
He mustered the courage, to utter a word,
Yet just as he did, they yelled "Hey there's the nerd!"

The Almond was sad, so he stumbled away,
What could he do, hide or just pray?
He suddenly realized, he'd always be alone,
He wished he were born, a leaf or a stone.

On his way back, a Walnut caught sight,
Of the Almond's despair, he just wasn't alright.
So follow him he did, all the way to his home,
The Walnut said, "Hi! My name is Jerome!"

The Almond was stunned, someone cared about him?
His eyes lit up bright, no longer so dim!
He replied to Jerome, with an innocent smile,
"You noticed me, please stay for a while!"

So the two mixed nuts chatted, for hours and hours,
They spoke about everything, the sun and the flowers.
Jerome never once, saw the Almond as broken,
His new friend was special, he was a rare token.

Then came the talk, about the next competition,
Jerome sounded eager, he had much ambition!
He told the small Almond, "We'd make a great team!
Let's do good together and achieve the big dream!"

The Almond then asked, "What could I possibly do?
I was born incomplete, you're sounding cuckoo!"
But Jerome saw past it, he believed in their bond,
He said, "Together, we can go, above and beyond!"

Jerome was so cheery, his spirit unbroken,
The Almond listened, to each word he had spoken.
"What could we do?", he asked his new friend,
To which Jerome said, "With me, you can blend!"

And so the Almond brought back, a honey jar and a spoon,
He'd never had so much fun, what a pleasant afternoon!
Jerome looked at the jar, and then dove in head first,
The Almond was amazed, at the Walnut's quick burst!

Honey-drenched Jerome approached his sidekick,
"If you stand really close, then we'll surely stick!"

The Almond came near, ready to get snug,
He opened his arms, and landed a hug.

The honey was their glue, they were bound as a pair,
Two different nuts, one heart they would share.
The next day it was time, to head to the town,
And show all the nuts, they deserved the real crown!

To the spectators' surprise, the two showed up combined,
They had done something foreign, to everyone's mind!
Pistachios and Pines, Hazelnuts and Pecans,
They were dazzled by the sight, like a lake filled with swans!

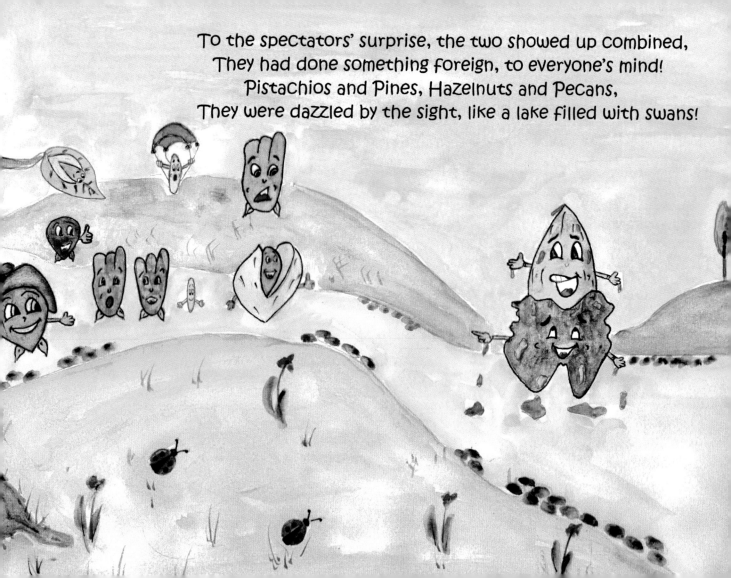

In an instant, an applause broke from the stands,
Congratulations were in order, many shook their sticky hands.
They were placed under the sun, for the roast to take place,
All eyes made their way, to the Almond's thrilled face.

Against all the odds, and with only one believer,
The Almond became, the town's greatest achiever.
He had used what he had, in the best way he could,
To be the first-ever 'Walmond', a treat that's so good!

Made in the USA
Las Vegas, NV
04 January 2025

15757446R20019